MACKINNONS' HOPE

A HIGHLAND CAROL

TANYA ANNE CROSBY

This one is still for Henry, my littlest love.

SERIES BIBLIOGRAPHY

These books are ALSO AVAILABLE AS AUDIOBOOKS

START WITH THE MACKINNON'S BRIDE FREE

THE HIGHLAND BRIDES

The MacKinnon's Bride

Lyon's Gift

On Bended Knee

Lion Heart

Highland Song

MacKinnon's Hope

THE GUARDIANS OF THE STONE

Once Upon a Highland Legend

Highland Fire

Highland Steel

Highland Storm

Maiden from the Mist

ALSO CONNECTED...

Angel of Fire

Once Upon a Kiss

DAUGHTERS OF AVALON

The King's Favorite

A Winter's Rose

Fire Song

Rhiannon

MEDIEVAL SCOTLAND

"'Celtic' of any sort is, nonetheless, a magic bag, into which anything may be put, and out of which almost anything may come. ... Anything is possible in the fabulous Celtic twilight...

— J.R.R. TOLKIEN

PART I
THE MACKINNON'S BRIDE

Mackinnons' Hope is a super-epilogue, meant to complement The MacKinnon's Bride and bridge The Highland Brides and Guardians of the Stone to the new series Daughters of Avalon. For your best enjoyment, please start with Book 1 of the Highland Brides

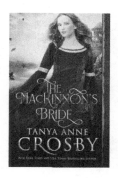

Free Download

PART II
MACKINNONS' HOPE

A HIGHLAND CHRISTMAS CAROL

PROLOGUE

Northumbria, Aldergh Castle, December 6, 1135
"In the name of the deceased, lady Eleanore of Aldergh, dead this sixth day of December in the year of our lord 1135..."

Hugh FitzSimon hurled the newly arrived letter across his desk. *Eleanore, dearest Eleanore, was dead.*

He'd kept her from their daughter all these years, never revealing to Page that her mother still lived. Why, he couldn't say, but now that Eleanore was gone, the knowledge settled like a stone in his breast.

To make matters worse, King Henry was calling all his barons to Lyons-la-Foret in France and Hugh could not bear to face that man—sovereign king or nay—especially not now. Thankfully, his bastard son, Afric, offered to save him the trip, representing Aldergh in FitzSimon's name.

It wasn't as though King Henry could be dying.

Howbeit, Eleanore, his dearest Eleanore, was gone, dead —her spirit flown to God.

Grief choked him.

Grief. Shame. Regret.

These would be his bedfellows now.

"Eleanore," he whispered low—a broken sound that bounced off bare stone.

His wife had been a vision, so lovely to behold. That she'd found it in her spirit to say nay to their king had simply never appealed to Hugh's sense of reason. After all, who could say no to their sovereign and protector? Hugh himself would have allowed the man to bugger him if he'd only but asked. But it made no sense to him that his meek little wife could hold her marriage vows above the wishes of their king. And despite the fact that she'd sworn she'd remained true, Hugh never found it in his heart to believe her—or to forgive her. And why? Because she'd caught Henry's eye?

Some part of Hugh had been envious as well.

It was true.

All his life he'd aspired to become more than a lowly baron. And then he'd gone and wed the lovely Eleanore, and King Henry suddenly took notice, inviting them both regularly to court, but his attentions were always for Eleanore, none for Hugh.

Out of jealousy, Hugh had cast his lovely bride aside, and pride never allowed him to bring her home. Even now, they would entomb her near the priory, and he would never again behold her lovely face.

And worse—for all the pain he'd caused, he'd made their daughter pay.

The last time he'd attempted to see Page, the MacKinnon threatened to cut out his heart. And that man would do it; Hugh had very little doubt. Iain MacKinnon was not a man to be trifled with.

Ultimately, this was all King Henry's fault, Hugh decided, but at least he wasn't alone in his misery. The King himself had no heirs. Henry's one and only son had found his fate at the bottom of the sea, leaving the king no choice but to name his daughter as his heir. Hugh might do the same for Page, except that she loathed him still.

A memory crept back to torment him, words that could never be recalled: *"My son for your daughter,"* MacKinnon had offered, tossing Page's shoe up onto the ramparts for Hugh to behold as proof that he held his daughter for ransom.

Hugh's heart had remained cold. *"What need have I of that brat?"* he'd said. *"I've sons aplenty and the means to forge myself more."* All bastards, not a one fit to bear his name. And yet, he'd declared, *"Keep her, or kill her. I care not which."*

And so MacKinnon kept her, and then he'd wed her, and FitzSimon never saw Page again.

A rumble of a sigh escaped him, the sound amplified in the cavernous interior of his home. What good were riches if they would be heaped upon his grave? What good was gold to a miserable sack of bones?

Aye, in truth, FitzSimon rued the day he'd sent his women away, for now who remained? He was alone, save for Afric, who only stayed because he hoped Hugh would enfeoff him—another bastard son to bear the Fitz name. Afric would be known as Afric Fitzhugh FitzSimon—hardly a legacy to be proud of!

Outside, the wind raged like a wailing banshee, sending furious howls into the castle through cracks in the walls. FitzSimon hadn't bothered with a fire in the hearth tonight. Why should he? He wore a fine, heavy cloak, lined with ermine—as splendid as any cloak worn by any king. Someday, it would be moth bait in a forgotten coffer somewhere, left to be picked over by wastrels who'd come to steal his remnants.

Heart heavy and despairing, he peered out the solar window, into the courtyard below. It was deserted now, as so many of his wards had abandoned him already to spend the winter with their families.

Afric, too, would soon be leaving for France. But Hugh was glad for that, because he did not enjoy Afric's companionship. He, like his common mother, reeked vulgarly of cloves.

Cursing softly beneath his breath, FitzSimon moved across the chamber, plucking up the odious parchment from his desk. One of the paperweights rattled carelessly across the desktop and rolled, falling with a rude clatter upon the wooden floor.

Still cursing, he rolled the parchment furiously, eyeing the burning taper on his desk, prepared to burn the letter. Something like tears burned at the back of his eyes. Sobs constricted his throat.

Forsaken.

That's what he was.

Be damned if he would allow himself to grieve over the loss of a woman who'd never loved him true.

At least that's what he told himself and that's what he was determined to believe. Fueled by a fresh rush of anger, he bent to blow out the taper.

What need had he of light when he knew every corner of this mausoleum? He had paced it from end to end for far too many years. And now, the castle was devoid of life—not a soul to happen upon, trip over, or even send scurrying back to their beds.

Muttering still more curses, Hugh stuffed the missive into his belt, deciding to put it away in a safe place, and he spun toward the solar door. His bed summoned him now, beckoning like a whore to his crackling bones. He made quickly for the door, stopping short at the sight of a shadow squirming there.

"Papa?"

Hearing the familiar voice, FitzSimon clutched at his chest, blinking to dispel the image of a little girl, her features growing clearer by the second.

"Papa?"

Could it be? But nay! It was a child, her face gaunt with sunken cheeks. Did they not feed her well enough? He smacked his breast to see if he might be dreaming in his bed. The whack he gave himself knocked the air from his lungs.

"Page?"

The girl's tiny form hugged the threshold, as though she feared Hugh might rip her free of her support and haul her away by the scruff of her neck. "I'm afeared, Papa" she said.

In times past, Hugh might have scolded the girl for presuming such a familiarity with him, because she was *not* his daughter—or so he'd once believed. Confused now, he rubbed his eyes and stuck a finger in his ear.

His daughter—no, what appeared to be his daughter—lingered in the threshold, her image a shimmery visage from his past. He asked her, "Why art afeared?"

The little girl, illumed by a strange blue aura, not unlike the blue heat of a flame, persisted in the doorway. "I cannot sleep, Papa. The wind wails, and my pillow is too thin."

Now he could clearly see the features of the girl's face, illuminated by that strange blue light. She looked *exactly* like Page at that age. "Your pillow's too thin?"

"Aye, sir."

Surely this child could not be his daughter? Page was fully grown by now, with children of her own. "Gads, child! What would ye have me do about the bloody wind? It seems to me ye'd do better to go and seek your prayers."

The child's face fell. "But... I cannot sleep, Papa."

"Aye, well, you should not be here," FitzSimon scolded her. "I've no idea what you be doing in my home. So shoo, now! Shoo! Shoo! Be gone!"

For a moment, the child's expression appeared crestfallen,

and then her mouth twisted into a disheartened moue, but she did not cry.

Of course, Page *never* cried. He remembered that stoic expression only too well. Even now it left Hugh with a guilty pang.

Disgusted, as much with himself, but no less with the child for having given him a prick of guilt, FitzSimon stamped his foot at the girl, as though she were naught but vermin skulking in his home.

The child turned and fled. Hugh made to chase her, but he stopped when her strange blue light extinguished amidst the dark hall. He stared down the corridor, not entirely relieved that she was gone. Strange as it was he could still hear her little footsteps echo down a distant hall.

"Rats," he muttered to himself. ""Tis naught but rats."

God's truth, he'd never touched a drop of *vin* this eve— not one drop. After all, what fun was there in drinking all alone?

Scratching his head, he reached for the parchment at his belt, and finding it still there, he patted it neatly and kept marching down the hall, all the more determined to find his bed.

His feet felt fat tonight, his toes swollen in his boots. His eyes burned. His gut churned, and it felt much the same as though some fat boar were seated upon his chest.

Outside, the wind bellowed harder, the sound all the more unnerving for the uncanny silence now ringing through his halls—a silence that grew, piercing his eardrums, and making him wince with pain.

By the rood, he did not feel well tonight.

It must have been that greasy pheasant! Rubbing his ears with the palms of his hands, he massaged them to ease the ache. But then, after removing his hands from his ears, he heard a woman's song in a faraway voice...

turned, and evidently forgotten amidst the weeds. He couldn't quite read the inscription. But behind that tomb lay row upon row of his ancestors' graves, none lay next to his, and none in advance of it. Beyond that last gravestone were only wicked looking briars.

"Tis cold," he complained, giving the ghost a sideways glance.

Eleanore smiled a knowing smile. "Colder yet ye'll find ye be, Hugh FitzSimon, but I shall give ye sunshine if 'tis what ye please."

Without ever moving Hugh found himself in a place he'd not visited in many years: *Chreagach Mhor*. It was springtime now—but how could that be?

Children laughed along the bluff-side, racing through rows and rows of dancing blue bonnets. *One. Two. Three. Four.* They came running past—and through him. One little boy ran directly through Hugh, laughing as he ran.

Hugh spun about to watch them race away, toward an old stone keep at the top of the hill—the ancient seat of the MacKinnon lairds.

Soaring high upon a gently sloping hill, *Chreagach Mhor* was a rugged fortress seated upon a violet mantle. The heather bloomed a brilliant violet against a vivid carpet of green and scattered across the lush landscape, rugged stones stood like proud sentries to guard the mammoth tower. Small thatch-roofed buildings spattered the hillside.

Another boy came racing past, perhaps this one no more than twelve. "Mother says to come along," he shouted at the escaping girls. "Tis time to sup."

The girls all squealed as the boy reached the hindmost runner, trying in vain to grasp the little girl's golden hair.

"Constance!" the boy screamed, when the child managed to evade him, and then all the girls laughed and scurried away.

Was this some form of hell, to glimpse a life he was never privy to?

Once again, Hugh FitzSimon slapped his burdened chest. "Dear Lord, Eleanore! Am I already dead?"

In truth, he did not feel so well this eve.

Eleanore smiled yet again, not quite warm, though not quite cold. Hugh could barely look at her for the brightness of her eyes. "Not yet, Hugh. Not yet."

And then they were no longer standing upon the hillside. They were in a barren field. It was sunny still, but now it seemed they'd somehow happened into the middle of a celebration, surrounded by happy folk the likes of which Hugh had never beheld.

His wife reappeared by his side, again, not alive, not quite dead. "Is this for real?" he asked. "What of ye? What do ye be?"

The blue glow in Eleanore's eyes dimmed—just enough so that he could spy the true color of her eyes: hazel green. "For love of ye, I come bearing gifts."

Hugh screwed his face. "From beyond the grave?"

Eleanore nodded, looking more like herself than the specter she had been. "Love, you see, is quite the hopeful thing."

Hugh remained confused. "B-But I did not love ye well enough!" he confessed.

"This I know."

"And yet ye loved me still?"

She nodded again and bade him to look about once more, so he could see what she had brought him there to see.

And there she was—his daughter, Page. Older now, with soft tendrils of sun-kissed hair framing a lovely grown-up face. After all these many years, she'd kept her beauty—just like her lady mother. But Hugh peered from mother to daughter, and realized with a start that Page had more of him than she had of Eleanore.

She had his face, not her lady mother's.

Amazed by the sight of his estranged daughter, he watched her hug a little girl—his granddaughter, Hugh supposed. And then another child came to tug her skirts. With a smile, Page bent to meet the little girl's gaze. The two spoke at length, after which the child hugged her neck and went racing away, laughing with unrepressed joy. By now, Hugh's heart pained him immensely. He could watch no more.

Dear God, he could watch no more!

Cruelly, Eleanore pushed him closer.

He glided uphill, all the easier to eavesdrop on his daughter's conversation with her laird husband. At first, Hugh was afeared they might spy him.

"You spoil them overmuch," Iain complained.

Hugh waved a hand before their faces. It swished through the air nebulously, passing through the MacKinnon's short gray beard.

They could not see him.

"And why not?" Page asked her laird husband, who by the way, had kept a hand about her waist, as though he could not bear the thought of losing touch. "I will not treat my children the way my father treated me."

Page's words were like daggers cast unerringly at Hugh's heart. He writhed a bit in pain.

The MacKinnon drew his wife close. "There is little danger in that, my love."

"A single tart for each will surely not break us," Page maintained, and then she cast her husband a worried glance. "Do you think there'll be enough to last the winter long?"

"Dinna worry, Page. The winter will be gone afore ye

know it, and then come spring we'll fill our stores. We'll find a way. We always do."

Hugh turned to Eleanore and whispered, "What happened here?"

Eleanore placed a finger to her lips, bidding him listen awhile longer.

Hugh glanced about the field, realizing suddenly that he was standing, not in the middle of a celebration as he'd originally imagined, but in the midst of men and women hard at work, rebuilding barns and clearing fields—and yet their smiles and laughter were scarcely dimmed by this fact. The summer blue bonnets were all dead now. The ground was brown and charred. And yet men and women joked and laughed and traded barbs.

Fire?

"Good day to ye, my lady," said a woman passing by.

"And to ye," Page greeted the woman with a wave.

"Bless ye mistress for givin' my girl a tart."

"'Tis my pleasure," Page assured the woman, and then she said beneath her breath, so that only her laird husband might possibly hear, "If only everyone were so easily pleased." Nibbling pensively at her bottom lip, she turned her gaze across the meadow. After a moment, she asked her husband, "What shall we do about him?"

Hugh followed his daughter's gaze and found her watching a young man, hard at work, lifting up beams for a peasant's roof. "It pains me to see him so at odds."

"For that, we may thank your Da," the MacKinnon suggested.

Hugh's cheeks burned hot.

What had he done now? Of course, he would be their demon, their ogre. He was the monster who stole in at night to steal little children from their beds—

Except that he had.

Not Hugh precisely, but of course, he was the one who'd detained young Malcom for the king. FitzSimon studied the youth a bit closer, realizing with a start that he recognized the face. It belonged to none other than the child he'd once harbored within his home.

Malcom MacKinnon worked side by side with his kinfolk, his shoulders shaped by the weight of too many heavy loads. He was a strapping young lad, Hugh thought— just the sort of man he'd always envisioned to take his place as lord of Aldergh. Too bad he was not of Hugh's blood.

How much time had passed? He counted upon his fingers. Eleven years since the day he'd cast his daughter away. Ten since he'd last beheld her face. And Malcom, he must now be seventeen.

His gaze sought and found the children across the field. They were all seated together, shoving sweet tarts into their faces. His gaze returned to his daughter—the child he'd denied for far too long. He longed to hold her in his arms. Had she ever in her miserable childhood enjoyed a single sweet tart? He didn't know, couldn't recall.

His throat felt too thick to speak, and yet he tried. "Do they have *enough—*" clothes, food, what else— "to last the winter long?"

Eleanore slowly shook her head.

"What will they do? What happens now?"

Without a word Eleanore swept her hand along the landscape, and suddenly they were standing in the very same field at twilight. The hillside had fallen silent; no laughter echoed through the meadow. He had the sense that many, many years had passed. The landscape was much changed. Like Aldergh, the castle on the hill stood no more. Stone by stone it had been dismantled, until all that remained was a stone footprint upon the hill, guarded by half turned stones. The land was barren, overgrown with thistle. The barns were gone. No more peasant homes remained.

Were their fates somehow entwined?

Hugh reconsidered the gravestone on Chapel Hill—and then, as though he'd conjured it, he was standing over the tombstone yet again, with Eleanore flickering like a candle by his side. He shivered beneath a gentle snowfall. A single flake fell upon his beard. Beside him, his pale dead wife wept a crystal tear. It fell to the ground, melting into the snow. Hugh peered down at the tombstone lying disfigured at his feet, one corner lopped off as though someone had taken a hammer to the stone. The words it bore finally brought him to his knees…

Etched in soft stone—not even deep enough to endure the years—was carved: Here lies Hugh FitzSimon, last heir of Aldergh Castle. The year engraved upon the stone was 1135, the month, December.

Eleanore spoke softly beside him. "*Knowing* is my gift, Hugh. While there is breath there is hope…"

Panic seized him. "What must I do? Tell me! What must I do!" He lifted his hands in supplication. "Anything, Eleanore, please tell me what to do!"

Much diminished now, Eleanore's light appeared weaker. She touched his shoulder so delicately that Hugh might have mistaken her touch for a snowflake.

"Before the fire burns low in the last hour of the last day before the winter solstice, you must change your heart, Hugh FitzSimon."

"'Tis changed, Eleanore! I *am* changed. Which fire? Please! Tell me, please?"

Eleanore spoke softer yet as she began to fade away. "Unattended, love is like a flame, burning lower day by day."

"Eleanore!" Hugh pleaded. She was barely visible now. He

reached out, trying to catch her to him, but his hands fell away from her translucent form, empty.

"You will know love when 'tis returned," she said, her voice drifting away.

And then Hugh was kneeling in the cold dark corridor of his home, left wretchedly alone.

His wife was gone.

Stricken with grief, he rose quickly from his knees in the empty silence of his hall and bolted into the solar.

Despite that he had already blown it out, the candle on his desk sat burning still, smoke curling up toward the ceiling as the tallow burned dirty and low.

What day is this?

Hurrying to the desk, Hugh pulled the newly delivered parchment from his belt, unrolled it swiftly and peered down at the writing, drafted in the studied hand of a Godly man. Illumined by the candlelight, the text changed before his eyes, as though written by some unseen hand. It now read:

"In the name of the deceased, lady ELEANORE OF ALDERGH Baron Hugh FitzSimon, dead this SIXTH twenty-second day of December in the year of our lord 1135..."

Was this a waking dream?

Behind Hugh, the hearth fire raged no longer, but there upon the floor laid the charred remains of his cloak. Proof that he was not mad. A sudden gust, like a ghostly sigh, lifted the ends of his wiry gray mane and the candle on the desk flickered softly. Hugh hurriedly cupped his hands about the candle flame, protecting it from going out.

Before the fire burns low in the last hour of the last day before the winter solstice, you must change your heart, Hugh FitzSimon.

"Do not forsake me, Eleanore!"

He had so much to do, so little time to do it!

CHAPTER 1

CHREAGACH MHOR, SCOTLAND,
DECEMBER 21, 1135

The fire drove them from their beds in the wee hours of the morn. The landscape raged, consuming crops and trees, setting fire to the night. Thankfully, it spared the majority of the villagers' homes, as well as the keep and some of the surrounding buildings. By the time the sun rose, all but one of the storehouses had been reduced to ash.

For nigh on a week, the clan had labored through a warm spell that would very soon end. Unseasonably warm, it afforded them a rare opportunity to work from sunrise and beyond sunset.

At seventeen, Malcom MacKinnon was as braw as any man, able to work his share and then some. So he did. As it was, theirs was an unforgiving land, in troubled times, and no Scotsman had the luxury of sitting about on his rear, ordering servants about. He'd witnessed such behavior only once in his life—many, many moons ago, while being held captive by Hugh FitzSimon. Thank God that his stepmother was naught like her odious Da.

He glanced in her direction, watching the way she swept around the site, providing drinks for thirsty men. She worked harder than any Highland lass, and harder yet than some of the men. Despite that she wasn't Malcom's true mother, she was nonetheless the light of his life. She could do no wrong—not in his eyes, nor in his father's.

Auld Angus spotted her, and the greedy sot tried to rise off his bench—no doubt to get himself another dram. But Page avoided the old man, and Malcom grinned.

God's truth, when it came to ale that old man had a tolerance like no other, but clearly, he'd had a bit too much. Angus claimed it loosened his joints, but from what Malcom could tell, it simply loosened his tongue. Page was gone long before he could manage to stand, and Malcom watched as he tried to get up, half hoping he wouldn't make it. Judging by the way that he wavered and fell upon his rear, he would be a liability returning to work.

Shaking his head, Malcom returned his attention to repairing the roof. So much damage had been done, still the mood was hopeful, and the help of their neighbors was appreciated.

In truth, he barely recalled a time when the clans were at war. Now it seemed more like than not that the Montgomerie brats were running about, stealing tarts from their windowsills and Brodie brothers were lolling about, draining his father's ale—and then their willies into the brambles.

Alas, the one thing that hadn't changed overmuch in all these years was that his maternal grandfather—Dougal MacLean—still kept to himself. He lived alone and would die alone—rumor was that he was on his deathbed, and it must be true, because Leith Mac Brodie had arrived without Alison.

Some part of him longed to go and see him, but he hadn't wanted much to do with Malcom in all these years, why would he care now, deathbed or nay? God's truth, he held a grudge worse than anyone Malcom ever knew and even Page had long ago forgiven her worthless father.

Even despite the fact that Old Man Maclean had made peace with his only remaining daughter, Alison, he couldn't seem to bring himself to extend that peace to Malcom or his family. Clearly, he still blamed Malcom's father for his eldest daughter's death, but rather than acknowledge that he'd had some part in Mairi's unhappiness, and that both Malcom and his Da were bound to share in his grief, he forsook them both. But there was no sense crying about it.

"Here," said Catrìona Brodie. "Take this to your father."

Not "please take this to your father." Just "take this to your father"—as though Malcom were a wee brat to be told what to do. He eyed her with a lifted brow, but threw down his shovel and took the rolled parchment from her hands, wondering what his Da would think when he handed him yet another revision to his blueprints.

Catrìona, like Page, worked harder than most of the men, but she was a bossy wench, taking over their crews from the instant she'd arrived. In truth, she could weave a thatch roof tight as you please and she could design with greater skill than most draftsmen, but he couldn't help but wonder what sort of clan raised a lass to work like a man—and to act like one too. Annoyed, he nevertheless started down the hill, considering the way Catrìona treated her husband—the same way she treated Malcom. "Do this. Do that," she would say. And Gavin would rush to do her bidding, all the while grinning like a *bampot*, as though he believed it would gain him some noteworthy prize. When it came time for Malcom to be wed, he sure didn't plan to marry anyone so bossy as Catrìona. But the way things were going, he was never going to be married. There was no one within leagues that even caught his fancy, and he had a yen to be away—somewhere where he could begin to matter.

Here he was only the MacKinnon's son, waiting for his father to die before he could begin his life, and the truth of that didn't set so well with him. He didn't know what he wanted out of life, but it was something more than this...

Riders came loping up the hill and all his grumblings were forgotten as he hastened to his father's side, handing him the parchment from Catrìona.

His father turned the document in his hand. "What's this?"

"From Cat," Malcom said, frowning, fixing his gaze on the approaching riders. "She claims the chimney's better positioned to the middle of the roof."

"Does she?" his father said, stuffing the parchment into his belt to deal with later, his gaze returning to the riders. "Where are your sisters?" he asked warily.

"Down by the brook."

"Good," he said, casting Malcom a sidelong glance, and then he gave him a nod. "Tell Catrìona to come to the hall."

"Are ye gonna rebuke her, then?"

"Nay, son," his father said. But it wasn't until the riders were halfway up the hill that Malcom understood why: A wolf's-head banner snapped in the breeze—the standard of the dún Scoti.

Somewhere nearby stood the cairn Broc Ceannfhionn had built for his murdered kinsmen, very close to where he'd buried his Merry Bells, his sweet, faithful dog.

Holding the wagon reigns, he considered a brief detour— if for no other reason just to see if he could find it.

There were a number of *cairns* along the way to Chreagach Mhor. Most were not built by the hands of a seven-year-old child. He, more than anyone, understood what it felt like to see a village burn. Only for him, it was not a careless fire that was the cause for his loss, but a raid upon his people. So long as he lived, he would never forget the day his parents died... the scent of seared flesh, the haunting refrain of terrified screams. These were the things that tainted his most distant childhood memories.

A sliver of sunlight stabbed him in the eye, making his eyes water, and he turned away, casting his gaze back along his cavalcade, settling his sights on his beloved children. There was barely enough room for them amidst the food and supplies, but not a one of them ever complained.

Griffin was nine. Maggie was ten. His eldest, Suisan, was already twelve. Lara, at seven, was the spitting image of her mother, with bright red hair and soul-stirring green eyes.

He'd never told any of them how their grandparents had died... all they knew was that Broc's kinsmen perished under unfortunate circumstances and that this was how Broc had come to live with the MacKinnons. Iain and his father had embraced him as a child of seven, taking him into their fold, and this was something for which he would ever be grateful.

Seated next to him, Elizabet was lovely as the day they'd met, her curls aflame beneath the late afternoon sun. As though by instinct, she peered in the direction of the cairn— where Broc had first confessed his love for her. And after a moment, she met his gaze, guessing at his thoughts. "Only think on it awhile. If you still feel the need to share with the children, we can stop on our way home."

Broc nodded.

She said, more gently, "Perhaps of greater import than the way they died is the legacy you will leave in their names?"

Together, they peered back at their band of wee ones seated in the carts. His daughter Suisan was becoming such a young lady. For all the long, bumpy journey, she'd kept her siblings preoccupied, telling tales and playing games. All four children were perfectly content at the moment, prompting him to worry less about ancient history, and more about the state of affairs of *Chreagach Mhor*.

By all the accounts Broc had received, *Chreagach Mhor* lay in ruins and it pained him immensely to consider his laird—he would always think of Iain this way—in such dire straits. He himself had risen from the ashes of his own clan, but he had Iain to thank for this.

Deciding to leave the cairn for later, he clicked the reins, moving along, eager to see Wee Constance and meet the woman she had become. Of all the folks he'd left behind, he must admit, it was hardest of all to leave his young cousin, wildling that she was.

Beside him, Elizabet drew her heavy cloak about her shoulders, pinching a loose fabric from her dress. "I'd forgotten how long the journey could be," she complained.

And noting the weariness in her face, Broc nodded back toward the cart where their children rode. "Why don't you take a rest? You need not keep my company the entire way."

"I am fine," she said sweetly, though she lifted her chin defiantly. "If you can do it, I can do it," she said as she rubbed at her well-rounded belly. "You must have sores on your bottom, same as I."

Broc chuckled low. "Truly," he said, giving his wife's belly a glance. "Tell the little sprite we'll be arriving soon."

MUCH TO EVERYONE'S SURPRISE, AIDAN DÚN SCOTI ARRIVED with more than two-dozen strong backs to join the reconstruction. Each man saw to his own mount as Iain greeted the dún Scoti laird. It humbled him to know that a man like Aidan, who rarely left his vale, would come so far to help. Allies they might be, but they were hardly neighbors. And now, more than ever, Iain was coming to realize the true value of their brotherhood—a bond of seven noble clans that included the hill Scots, the MacLeans, the Montgomeries, the Brodies, and the last of the McNaught and MacEanraig clans.

All save for Jaime Steorling had come to offer aid, and Jaime, 'twas said, had been summoned to another of King David's councils—a summons that could not be ignored.

"I believe the last time you were here was for your sister's wedding," Iain reminded.

In fact, Aidan had born that situation nobly, for his sister had been ripped from the bosom of her kin by David of Scotia, with the sole purpose of bartering her to England—much the same as was done to his own son. But unlike Malcom, Catrìona had escaped her captors and promptly found herself a Brodie husband and protector.

Aidan arched a brow. "Aye, well, it took me all these years to get over the temper it left me in." He removed his riding gloves, tucking them into his waist, and said, "South was never my favorite way to ride."

Laughing, Iain clapped Aidan on the back. "I bid ye Welcome, my friend. No matter how many years go by, I am no less pleased to see you."

Both men sobered over that, for, indeed, too many years had passed. Both lairds were now sporting silver in their hair —Iain quite a bit more than Aidan.

"I would have brought more," Aidan said by way of apology, speaking of his men and the supplies they'd delivered, "Alas, the rest was needed in the Vale."

Dark days lay ahead. There were whispers of war in the air. David of Scotia was taking stock of his armies and his allies, eyeing Northumbria greedily, while Henry of England was in Normandy, fighting to secure his holdings. And if that were not enough, 'twas said that Henry's daughter's rebellions were beginning to take a toll on his health.

"We are eternally grateful for all ye could provide," Iain reassured. "Tis a generous offering, no less."

"'Tis the least we could do. And how is your lovely wife?"

"Page is well. What of Lìli?"

Aidan smiled. "We've a brand new bairn. 'Tis why she couldn't travel."

"Lucky bastard," Iain said, and gave him an elbow.

The manor was bustling. The men were all busy assembling tables in the hall while the women scrambled to find food enough to feed so many hungry mouths. Knowing Page as well as he did, Iain did not add feeding the masses to his list of concerns. Along with Glenna, his wife could make a fine soup from a pile of stones.

At the rear end of his hall, they climbed his stairs, the sound of their footfalls echoing behind them. "I hear tell Henry called his liegemen to France."

For a moment, Aidan let the announcement hang in the air, leaving Iain to mull over the possible reasons.

"Do you know why?"

Aidan shook his head. "All I know is that Steorling has gone to Edinburgh to meet with David. He took my brother and your nephew. I believe he means to offer them a position with his newly formed guard." He, meaning King David, Iain surmised. "As for Henry, your guess is as good as mine."

Displeased with the news of his nephew, Iain clenched his jaw. "I suppose it means we'll not have the pleasure of Cameron's company any time soon."

Cameron had left them years ago, and in his absence, his little sister Constance had grown into a young woman—a bit of a wildling at that. Iain dreaded the day she would come to him with a bairn in her belly and no husband to provide for her. "It's just as well he did not come," he said. "As it is, you and your men will be sleeping three men deep."

Aidan grinned. "Better three men deep than alone on

nights like these, eh? Never fear, my friend, ye'll hear no complaining from my men. We have not come to bring you more grief."

Once again, Iain clapped Aidan on the back. "Ye canna know how much it means to us, Aidan. Come now," he said. "Let me show ye where to settle your things."

He led the dún Scoti chieftain into his solar, where there were already quite a few pallets laid upon the floor. "This is where you will bunk your men."

And then he took Aidan to a tower room—one he'd used for himself many, many moons ago. After the death of his first wife, he'd kept the chamber locked and the windows boarded, but those burdensome memories were long gone. He no longer believed in ghosts.

Examining the scarcely furnished room, Aidan nodded appreciably. "This is far more generous than I would have hoped for," he said, and it struck Iain, not for the first time, that the dún Scoti chieftain was as humble a man as he'd ever known. "If you would but send a messenger to the Brodies," Aidan continued, but he barely got the words out of his mouth when Catrìona appeared in the doorway.

"Aidan!" she exclaimed.

Aidan spun about at the sound of his sister's voice, a grin splitting his face. His arms flew wide, beckoning her into his embrace and the lass fairly flew across the room, leaping like a wee child into her brother's arms.

Behind her came Iain's daughter Liana. She too was grinning widely. At ten years old, she was the image of her mother. "Papa!" she said, excitedly. "More wagons are coming! Mama says to tell you they bear Dunloppe's banners!"

A smile to match the dún Scoti's erupted over Iain's lips, for Broc Ceannfhionn was his oldest and dearest friend.

CHAPTER 2

E ven with a rising chill in the air and a shortage of
cloaks and blankets, there were hugs aplenty to go
around, followed by smiles and laughter. It was a heartfelt
reunion, despite that the reason for the gathering was no
cause for celebration.

Tonight's bonfire, like the one they'd burned the night
before, was an offering to Cailleach Bhuer, the blue-faced
mother of winter. They honored her in hopes that she would
continue to stave away winter snows—at least until their
reconstruction was complete. The huts they were rebuilding
now had frames, but they still had some ways to go.

For as far as the eye could see, the surrounding grass was
already charred, but Iain had given very specific instructions
for the building of their bonfire, so as to lessen any further
risk of fire. But, in spite of recent events, his kinsmen took
comfort in the night's celebration, for it was a keen reminder
that, from the darkest womb of night, light—and hope—was
born. Tonight, even despite their misfortunes, he felt like a
man well-blessed and ready to share. With so many folks in
attendance, he considered sending word to the MacLeans

and the Montgomeries, asking them to join, but it was hardly appropriate to invite a man to sup and ask him to bring his own vittles. Fortunately, the sentiment was moot, because Gavin Mac Brodie slipped away to raid his pantry yet again. And much to Ian's relief, he brought along Montgomerie as well. The lot of them arrived leading more donkeys overladen with supplies. The sight of them brought a sting to his eyes.

For clansmen who'd once lived amidst bitter feuding, his neighbors' unflagging generosity filled his heart.

His voice was thick with emotion as he greeted his guests with eager claps on the back. And once all the hellos were said, they hoisted a hog into the pit and set a table that would put a king's feast to shame.

The last time they'd had so many people all together, they were gathered to raise Dunloppe from the ashes—a gift to Broc Ceannfhionn from David of Scotia, in return for his oath of fealty. It was that one act of kindness that had prompted Iain to forgive and forget, and if he couldn't precisely bend the knee, he could give the man his due where he could. He only wished his son could let it all go. Alas, Malcom was an angry young lad, with no desire to forgive, much less forget.

And thankfully, not everyone was quite so hard-hearted. Auld Angus, with one black eye delivered by Catriona's knee, played his reed, a song he dedicated to Cat. The children scurried about, laughter quick to touch their lips as the sound of a few lingering hammers rang in the distance, a strange accompaniment to Angus' doleful song.

For the fourth or perhaps fifth time—who was counting? —Iain embraced his old friend Broc. "You're a sight for sore eyes," he said.

Broc hugged him back, unashamed to linger in his embrace. "Och, mon, di' ye think we would leave you to fend for yourselves? Nay, my dear friend, what's mine is yours to have."

Iain grinned, teasing. "'Tis a wonder ye've anything left at all with so many mouths to feed. Ye've been a busy, busy mon."

Broc laughed, crossing his burly arms, offering Iain a twinkle-eyed wink, his gaze drawn toward Aidan dún Scoti, who was now standing on the opposite side of the bonfire, speaking at length with his little sister. "I see ye've managed to lure *his majesty* from the Vale? How in God's name di' ye manage?"

Iain shrugged. "He came of his own accord, Broc. But ye ken I'd never ask."

"Aye, well, bastard—he's yet to meet my gaze even once since I arrived, even despite that his sister's pleased enough with her choice of husband. I dinna believe he'll ever forgive me for putting Lael in harm's way."

Nodding, Iain, too, crossed his arms. "He will in time, Broc. He's a good mon, and in truth, were it my sister ye took to war, even with all our many years together, I may have had trouble forgiving ye as well."

"Good thing ye haven't any sisters," Broc joked, and Iain barked with laughter.

"Look at it this way, Broc. He's not yet strangled ye yet, so I'd say 'tis progress, and, look, ye're both warming your fat arses 'round my fire."

Broc grumbled. "I dinna ken how much progress it is. Ye've gone and built the biggest bloody bonfire I ever did see." He shook his head in wonder. "The man could be warming his arse all night long and never see me once."

There was a lot of rubble to clear," Iain said, and sighed, as Page came wending her way through the crowd, swiping her long graceful fingers on her stained and dirty skirts.

stranger to their clan. It mattered not who his father was. Everyone was suspect to Malcom's way of thought.

"Tell me more about Dubhtolargg," he heard Constance say in a whisper, and Kellen scooted closer.

Malcom frowned as the dún Scoti boy waved a hand along an imaginary landscape, embellishing for the benefit of a girl. "Our vale is surrounded by mountains, ringed with rowan trees—almost as beautiful as your hair."

Malcom rolled his eyes and tried not to bark with laughter.

"My father's house sits on a loch."

Constance asked, aghast, "In the water?"

"On stilts. 'Tis called a *crannóg*," the dún Scoti lad said. He was a pretty little man with a silver tongue, and he looked nothing like his father.

"What happens when it storms? Does the water rise into your beds?"

"Never," the boy said. "This is the way my ancestors have lived for many, many years."

Constance bowed her head, looking at him coyly. "I would dearly love to see it someday."

"Perhaps you will?" Kellen said, resting a hand upon her knee and Malcom cleared his throat, very loudly.

Kellen started, spotting him at once, and withdrew the hand. Constance never even bothered peering about, and Malcom crossed his arms.

"What about your kinsmen?" she asked, completely enthralled. "Do they sleep beneath the same roof? How large your *crannóg* must be!"

Once again, Malcom rolled his eyes, quite sure Kellen would take it as a point of male pride—yet so long as it was only his *crannóg* they were discussing, Malcom couldn't be bothered to care.

"Nay," Kellen said, leaning back on one arm. "We have a village, same as ye."

Constance shivered, rubbing her arms.

"Are ye cauld, lass?"

"Just a bit," his cousin said, batting her long lashes. Och, but she had no idea how dangerous those sultry looks could be...

Perhaps sensing him, Kellen cast a wary glance in Malcom's direction and Malcom smiled thinly. So long as he stayed close, they were bound to behave, so he settled in for the duration and laid his head back to peer up at the countless stars, deciding to give his eyes a bit of rest and letting his ears do the work. Clearly, he had no notion how tired he was. He'd only meant to close his eyes for a moment. But he fell fast asleep, listening to the distant tap, tap, tap of persistent hammers.

CHAPTER 3

DECEMBER 22, 1135

Dawn broke over a smoky landscape.

The bonfire that had burned so brightly the evening before was now reduced to burning coals and ash.

Malcom awoke with a start.

Quick on the heels of the realization that he'd fallen asleep came the awareness that he was also the first to wake. The first pleased him not at all. The second filled him with relief, because everything and everybody—so far as he could see—was still in one piece.

The ground was covered with sleeping forms. Feet intertwined, arms and legs askew, heads over and beneath leaf-covered tartans. It was a veritable sea of sleeping folk, all wearing cherry-red noses from the cold and dirty cheeks from sleeping on half burnt grass.

He didn't spot Constance, and hoped she would have the good sense to go to her bed. He said a little prayer that it must be so. And then, rubbing at his eyes, he stumbled to his feet, realizing that the haze of the morning was more mist than smoke. Even now, the rising sun was burning the grey away, brightening the landscape. Yawning, he stretched, intending to go searching for Constance—and froze where he stood.

Nay.

It wasn't possible.

He rubbed his eyes and looked again.

It simply wasn't possible.

But there it was.

They were surrounded, not by half-finished homes, but by fully formed cottages, all with thatch roofs. For an instant, he wondered if some faerie had lifted him up and carried him to another place, but nay... there was auld Angus sprawled at his feet.

Mute with shock, he stepped over Angus, and with mouth agape, he moved soundlessly toward the closest hut, quite certain he must be dreaming, and that the cottage would vanish any second. "'Tis but a dream," he whispered to himself.

"What's that?" Angus mumbled. The old sot lifted his flash, but rather than bring it to his mouth, he brought his mouth to the flask, struggling to drink with swollen, eyes half closed.

Malcom didn't answer. He continued putting one foot in front of the other, stepping over sleeping kinsmen, until he reached the hut and splayed a hand against the newly erected wood.

It was perfectly solid, and yet, there was no way a few stubborn men with a handful of hammers could have so quickly completed what they'd begun a week ago. Last night, after the sun went down, these houses were still incomplete.

"What the devil?" he heard Angus ask.

And then another kinsman asked, "What in damnation?"

"The houses—look, Glenna, they've built themselves!"

"'Tis a gift from the Cailleach!" she said. "Or brownies!"

"Impossible!" he heard another man exclaim, but Malcom stood transfixed, examining the newly erected homes.

The Cailleach? *Would they truly have him believe some old crone waved a magik staff and produced all these homes?*

His pleasure over the discovery was fully dampened by the simple fact that all these cottages could not have been constructed without a *lot* of help. Someone had worked all night long, and unless every last guest put aside his *uisge* and ale, and then worked all night long whilst Malcom snored, there was simply no way this could have been done.

Startled by the discovery, his cousin was summarily forgotten. Malcom raced toward the keep to alert his Da.

CHREAGACH MHOR'S GREAT HALL HAD NEVER SEEN SUCH AN audience—not even during trials.

Presiding from his dais, Iain MacKinnon contemplated the surrounding faces. Quite possibly, everyone he knew was present here today, along with the lairds and families of all the neighboring clans. Some who did not fit inside the hall were listening from the courtyard.

His son stood before him on the dais, suspicion hardening his usually gentle features. "Someone was here, Da. Whoever it was might also responsible for our fire—I know it."

Iain stared at his firstborn. "There's no proof anyone set that fire, Mal, and if they had, why the devil would they burn our village, then rally to rebuild whilst we slept? It makes no sense."

Malcom gave a frustrated shake of his head, as though he too could not fathom the reasons behind such an act. "I dinna ken. All I know is I've a feeling down in my bones."

"I had a feeling down in my bone this morning, too," Angus quipped, and laughter erupted through the hall.

Iain shot the old man a quelling glance and Auld Angus had the good sense to look chagrined. "Sorry," he said, casting Malcom a contrite look.

Clearly annoyed by his father's unwillingness to listen, Malcom ignored the old man's apology. "Ye take me too lightly," he complained. "I've never cried wolf, Da."

That much was true. His son was not the sort to go running about half-cocked, spouting to everyone who would listen that the sky was falling. But Iain also realized that his son distrusted everyone he knew. He had no inkling how to relax amidst so many guests, and as usual, he was searching the shadows for traitors, watching in vain for betrayals. Alas, this truth had only worsened as he'd aged—but damned Glenna. That old bat only encouraged him with her talk of Cailleach and Brownies.

As close to an uncle as Malcom had, Broc stepped forward to place a hand on his son's shoulder. "Your Da has never taken you lightly, Mal," he said gently.

Malcom shrugged away. "What do ye know? You left us a long time ago!"

"Malcom!"

It wasn't often that Iain raised his voice and the occupants of the hall started, some retracting their necks into their shoulders. Broc stepped back, out of the way, looking pained.

Iain glowered at his firstborn child. "You'll not speak to your elders in such a manner. Do I make myself clear, son?"

Malcom barely nodded. Still, he said, "I'm sorry, Da." And he cast a short glance over his shoulder at Broc as well. "Sorry."

"No offense taken," Broc allowed.

Malcom turned once more to address his father, his

expression tormented. "I *know* something is amiss, Da. I feel it. Dinna ye ken?"

Iain sighed portentously, wondering what Malcom would have him do—dispatch the entire clan, along with their guests, to search the woods? Betimes his son did have a touch of the sight. After all, when he'd said he'd spied the Weeper, they lost a good friend. But somehow, that was different, and these were hard facts: The village burned a few days ago. No cause had yet to be found. It appeared to be but a random fire that had begun in precisely the wrong spot. But, even were the fire set apurpose, there could be no rational explanation for or any connection to the sudden and immediate completion of their homes. One simply did not amount to the other... inasmuch as the two events could not be connected—at least not in his measured opinion—it was nevertheless a mystery as to how so much work could have been completed in so little time.

"Did anyone see anything at all?" he asked the crowd at large.

A sea of faces peered back at him, head shaking. "Not I," said a few.

"Nor I."

"We heard hammers all night, but we dinna think to check to see who was working."

"It was *bodachan sabhaill*!" suggested Glenna, changing her mind about the Cailleach, and raising her hand.

Iain furrowed his brow. The last time she'd claimed there was a haunting in their barn, it turned out to be none other than Aidan's sister Catrìona, who'd stolen a palette of their candles. Thankfully, that was all in the past and no brownies had ever been spied during his lifetime.

"It was not *bodachan sabhaill, or Cailleach, or the Weeper*," said Iain, frowning.

And yet, someone *had* finished the work—someone who

perhaps wished to help, but who did not want thanks. They had a large company of new faces—certainly more than enough people to have seen the job done if they'd so pleased, but no matter how hard he looked, no one seemed the least inclined to step forward and take credit for the work. Nor, in truth, did Seana's *uisge* ever inspire such acts. "No one?" he asked again.

Finally, one man did step forward, raising his hand. "Laird!" shouted someone at the back of his hall.

Iain turned to spy Kerwyn shouldering his way through the crowd. He was dragging in a shamefaced Constance behind him, hair mussed and filled with bits of straw.

"Constance?" Iain asked.

Kerwyn said, "Your lovely niece has something she would like to say…"

Iain frowned. That's all he needed right now—to hear the lass had gone and bedded one of their guests. The merest thought turned his gut.

Looking entirely too contrite, the lass stumbled forward, and Iain mentally counted all the available lads she might have seduced. At once, he cast a glance at Aidan dún Scoti, searching for his young son. To Iain's memory, Kellen was the one his niece seemed most drawn to—by God, he didn't have to look far. Behind Kerwyn and Constance came the dún Scoti lad, dragged into the hall by the scruff of his tunic.

Iain whispered prayer for strength.

Aidan dún Scoti's hands fell away from his chest, his eyes rolling backward, his jaw turning taut.

"Constance—what in Cailleach's name ha'e ye done, lass?"

She had been weeping, Iain could see. Red-eyed and pink nosed, she swiped tears from her cheeks with a trembling thumb.

For his part, Kellen dún Scoti had the good sense to remain silent, despite the manhandling he received, and thankfully, his father remained where he stood, frowning though he was.

The hall fell silent as both youths were brought before Iain—neither a day past sixteen. Iain sighed and cast another wary glance at the boy's father. To the dún Scoti's credit, he merely nodded, giving Iain leave to rule as he wished, though he crossed his arms again, none too pleased.

"We found 'em sleeping in the stable," Kerwyn announced.

Iain leveled Kellen a stern look, and another for Constance. "Is this true?" he asked.

Constance nodded, swallowing her tears. "Aye, but we were sleeping," she said, with a watery hiccup.

God save them all.

Iain regarded the state of her dress and the bits of straw in her hair, and realized that even if this were true, her reputation would be ruined. No decent man would have the girl now if he thought she'd given her maidenhead so easily. He saw visions of Constance running about as a dirty old maid, lifting her skirts for all the married men to see—not that she would ever do so, mind you. She had long outgrown the need to show everyone her lily-white arse, and yet the image plagued him nonetheless. He turned to address Kellen. "How old are you, lad?"

To his credit, the boy's gaze never faltered. "Sixteen, laird."

Iain remained silent, contemplating what best to do. He tapped his fingers angrily on the arm of his chair, looking first at Broc, then again at Aidan.

"We didn't do anything," Constance wailed, shrugging free of Kerwyn's constraints. "Let me go," she said defiantly. "Ha'e ye not embarrassed me enough?"

Iain rubbed his brow wearily. The mystery of the huts properly forgotten for the time being, he gave his niece his full regard. Unfortunately, there was only one way to handle this matter and he feared it might come to blows. Already, Aidan dún Scoti had lost a sister to their clans, and now he stood to lose a son… little wonder he didn't leave his vale.

And, if Aidan rued the thought of losing one more of his kinsmen to their clan—it may not bode so well.

His voice was deceptively soft when he spoke. "Get out everyone," he commanded. "Out," he said. "All save the boy and his Da."

"And you!" he said to Constance when she suddenly made to leave. He pointed a finger at her.

"Da!" Malcom exclaimed, realizing that Iain meant for him to leave as well.

"Out," he told his son. "This does not concern you, Mal."

Malcom scowled. "Only gi' me two men to search the woods," he begged. "I'll not bother you again. And if there is naught to be found I will speak of it no more."

"Malcom," Iain said tightly. "Dinna try me, son. We have no cause to believe there is aught amiss here, and the men have all worked too hard. Please go."

Malcom stood stubbornly, glaring at his father.

"Now," Iain said.

As the crowd disbursed, Aidan moved forward, and finally, Malcom turned to go, casting Iain a baleful glance as the dún Scoti laird came to stand behind his son. Thankfully, his son said naught more, but he marched down the steps, his hands forming fists by his sides and Iain spewed another sighed.

His only son and rightful heir was nearly a man now, fueled by the fears of a child. God's truth, he felt more comfortable with the notion of passing his legacy to his daughter. At least he knew Liana had an even temper and a level head. He watched Malcom go, torn between his unwavering love for his firstborn child and fear for the future of his clan. Only once Malcom gone did he turn to address the youths presented before him.

"I stand by whatever judgment you make," Aidan said firmly, and Iain felt a surge of relief.

But Kellen had no need to turn to look at his father to speak. He peered up at Iain and said, "I love her and will wed her here and now, if you please."

CHAPTER 4

"Great gods who create and bring forth life, we ask your blessing on this day of celebration."

A sea of faces stared up at the wedding couple, but Kellen's mother was not among them to see her firstborn take his vows. Aidan imagined all the possible ways he could die at his wife's hands. She was an accomplished alchemist, and with Una's help, she was bound to know a few ways to make him suffer before he departed this life.

For his part, Kellen looked more pleased than he had a right to. The lad stood next to his bride, grinning hugely. The girl was but fourteen, Kellen sixteen, and both were little more than babes to Aidan's eyes.

He remembered the day Kellen arrived at Dubhtolargg, with his deep, inquisitive eyes. He'd given the boy a safe haven, and as a result Kellen had lived a far less guarded life than most youths. He had to remind himself that his own parents were already wed by this age—the difference being that, neither of these two young people met before yesterday, and he couldn't help but worry over their future.

Perhaps Lìli would see it as a boon that he was bringing

home another soul to love. And it could be worse; he could be leaving Kellen here as he had Cat.

"You will join hands," the old woman called Glenna commanded the pair.

Eager to see the ceremony over and done, both Kellen and Constance rushed to do the woman's bidding. As he watched them, Aidan was forced to confess: They looked quite pleased with the turn of events.

Glenna held in her hand a number of ribbons and she looped one over their joined wrists, binding them together, as Una had once done for Aidan and for Lìli. The memory brought a wistful turn to his lips and he longed to hold his wife.

"Constance and Kellen, do ye come forward of your own free will to make this union?"

"I do," said Kellen loudly enough for everyone to hear.

"And you, Constance?" the auld woman asked.

"I do!" she replied happily. The excitement in her voice was genuine and Aidan recognized the look of love —or if not love, precisely, the seeds of love. Nurtured properly, it would grow into something glorious and extraordinary.

Now Glenna looked to the boy's uncles—Broc and Iain, respectable lairds in their own rights. He could do worse than to be bound by blood to these men.

Each man gave a nod. And then Glenna peered toward Aidan and Aidan offered the same. The old woman gave a nod in return, acknowledging their grace.

For better or worse, their union was blessed, and if these two young folks would not deal well with one another, they would discover it soon enough.

Dressed in a pale blue dress, with goldenrod and sage in her hair, Constance looked radiant and resolved.

"This binds you together for one year and one day,"

Glenna explained. "During this time, Constance and Kellen, will you honor and respect one another?"

"I will," said the pair in unison.

The old woman then wrapped another ribbon about their wrists and continued, "Will you forever aid each other in times of pain and sorrow?"

"I will," both said once more, and again, the old woman looped another ribbon about their joined wrists.

"Will you be true to one another that you may grow strong together?"

"I will," Kellen said at once.

"I will," agreed Constance. She gave Kellen a lover's glance, albeit one filled with such innocence that Aidan realized his son had spoken truth. Kellen had not yet bedded this girl. The two had simply hidden away to do what young folk were bound to do—whisper sweet nothings into one another's ears and maybe steal a kiss or two.

"As your hands become withered, will you reach only for each other?" the old woman continued, and Aidan wondered if Kellen realized what she'd meant—not only that he must he confide in his new bride, forsaking all others, but he must never swing his willie near other lassies. Thankfully, Kellen was his mother's son, kindly and respectful of others. But he vowed to have himself a long-overdue talk with the boy.

"We will," said the two in unison, and for a fourth time, the ribbon was looped about their wrists.

"Is it your intention to bring peace and harmony to these united clans?"

"It is."

"When you falter—and you shall—will you have the courage—and loyalty—to remember these promises you have made to one another?"

"I will," Kellen said, smiling brightly.

"With all my heart," Constance agreed, and she gave

Kellen a smile that brought a grin to Aidan's face as well. The sight of the two warmed the cockles of his heart.

"Verra well, " Glenna declared, "Constance and Kellen, as your hands are now bound, so too are you bound to one another. Kellen, you may bestow a kiss of peace upon your bride."

Timidly at first, looking toward Aidan and then to Broc and then to Iain—as though he were asking for permission— Kellen leaned in with puckered lips. But he closed his eyes and when his lips touched his bride, they missed their mark. He planted a chaste kiss on her eye. To the girl's credit, she merely smiled.

The gathering laughed, but quietly.

Red-faced, Kellen reached out to hold his bride's cheeks, as though to keep her still for his kiss and then, with eyes wide open, he gave the kiss another try. Before he could accomplish his mission, Constance thrust out her hands, pulling her new husband close—much too quickly and the two knocked chins, moving away from each other with startled yelps.

The gathering laughed yet again, and a few old men not so politely as before.

Finally, Kellen pulled his bride into his arms, kissing her sweetly, lips still closed, and Aidan shoulders shook with mirth.

Finally, quite pleased with himself, his son turned to raise their bound arms for everyone to see and a cheer rang out through the crowd. That swiftly and thoroughly the handfasting was over. The sound of music lifted, and Kellen embraced his bride, twirling her around and around.

"She's a lovely lass," Catrìona whispered at his side.

Aidan turned to look at his youngest sister, marveling over how well the years had treated her. Her hair was still full of lively red curls, and her cheeks were blooming. "That she is," he agreed, taking her arm into his, and pulling her near so he could whisper in her ear. "And what of you, Catrìona? Are ye still so pleased with your mon?"

She nodded very quickly, and Aidan peered over at his brother by law. "'Tis a good thing ye've loved my sister well, Mac Brodie."

Arms crossed, eyes twinkling, Gavin chuckled. "Dinna think for one instant she would have it any other way, good man."

Aidan laughed over the truth of that. None of his sisters were weak or timid, he acknowledged.

With bawdy shouts, the crowd made way for Kellen and Constance as they moved down the hill, half dancing to the music as they went.

All banter was soon swallowed by the uproar. Ribald jibes followed the wedded pair. Little ones tossed late blooming flowers at their feet. Despite the haste, it had been a lovely wedding, and Aidan found himself clapping his hands as the festivities carried the pair toward the night's bonfire—a massive undertaking that had been built to honor the Mother of Winter. But tonight, it would honor the bride and groom as well.

Catrìona fell behind, walking with her husband arm in arm. "He likes you," Aidan heard her say, and he wanted to laugh, and put the man at ease, but it was quite enough that Cat could reassure him, and this much was true: he valued any man who could bring such unrepressed joy to his sister's heart, whether or not he might be an outlander.

CELEBRATING LIKE FILTHY PAGANS, NO ONE APPEARED TO CARE one whit that flames had destroyed half their village less than a week before. In his arrogance, the MacKinnon had ordered yet another bonfire, one that was bigger than the last.

Tonight's bonfire spat glowing cinders against a twilight sky as Afric watched the wedded go by.

Of course, young Malcom was right; something *was* amiss. And yet, had it been his intent to devastate the clan beyond reparations, he would have killed them all whilst they'd slept in their beds. But nay, he already had a long list of souls he should make amends for, and he had no desire to add to that list unnecessarily.

For now, there was only *one* person he wished to kill, and the fire had been a ruse to keep her within sight.

Earlier, as he'd stood in the hall—a stranger in their midst —listening to the laird's son attempt to convince his father that there was foul play at hand, Afric had worried his opportunities would be lost. But then, the MacKinnon dismissed the lad, and here they were, none the wiser—all but Malcom.

Of course, it was easy enough to believe all was right with the world when neighboring clans came together this way. For an instant, it left Afric with a guilty pang... but only for an instant. These were *not* his people and given the opportunity, they would mete him the same fate. Survival depended upon which side you were on—and Afric was most assuredly not on their side. But neither was he on Hugh's—stupid bag of wind.

Did Page believe their father's apathy was reserved only for her? Nay. He'd treated Afric as he did all his bastards—with very little regard, ordering him around like a common servant. He couldn't even be bothered to read his own letters —a fact for which Afric would be eternally grateful, because as yet, he still hadn't heard the news...

Now everything was going according to plan.

It was easy enough to hide amidst so many faces, old and new. Afric could come and go as he pleased. No one had any notion who he was, or whence he hailed. Even Hugh had yet to recognize him. But, of course, his father was a doddering fool, far too easily deceived. Whilst he'd run about gathering supplies and men for his journey north, Afric rode ahead, under the pretense of going to France. Instead, he'd come here, and set the stage to see his mission done. Once he was rid of his competition for Hugh's lands, and then Hugh, as well, he would go to claim his prize.

Smiling, despite the fact that they'd lost nearly all they, the clansmen all ate, drank and made merry, kicking up their heels, singing obnoxiously to the accompaniment of the pipes.

Oblivious.

Obnoxious.

Obligors.

Later, once they heard the news, all would pale in the face of it. Music would end in a discordant note. The skies would darken with the dimming of hope. The air would chill with heralding fate... Henry Beauclerc was dead—poisoned by his mistress, Morwen. Of course, this was not widely known, but Afric knew it, because King Stephen's son Eustace had told him.

King Stephen. He liked the sound of that as much as he did Lord Aldergh—his reward for keeping his mouth shut. His reward for providing that old witch a vial of poison. Those who did not know would think it the result of a number of bad eels, but Afric knew better.

Now, upon the king's death raged winds of war. Agents had been disbursed, like a sickness transmitted unto the lands. Thanks to Henry's beautiful witch, all pawns were now in place, and everyone who'd sworn fealty to Henry's shrewish daughter Matilda would meet their makers one by one—including the man who'd impregnated his mother.

Hugh FitzSimon.

At this very instant, the King's own nephew, Stephen of

Blois, was moving in to seize the throne and, in the utter chaos soon to follow, Afric would take his example and seize Aldergh for himself. Once his father was dead, there was no one to gainsay him except his estranged daughter, and soon enough not even Page...

Thinking of all the things he could change when he returned to his home as the rightful lord, he tamped his foot merrily as bride and groom came dancing near.

None of Hugh's men would think to question him when he seized control, for Hugh was as stingy as he was mean and one good turn for these Highlanders would not buy him indulgences with God.

"Long life to ye," he shouted at the happy couple, raising a toast to the pair.

Little did they realize it was a flout in their faces.

"Thank ye sir!" exclaimed the bride. She rushed over to kiss Afric upon the cheek, her breath warm and sweet.

All too easy, he thought to himself. *All too easy.* How fortuitous this would be... in one fell swoop he would be rid of father and daughter both.

"'Tis a right bonny pair they make, dinna ye think?"

Careful to hide his accent—for his mother had been a Frankish maid—Afric nodded to the man who'd spoken—the Montgomerie laird, for he wore the Lion-head livery beneath his blue tartan cloak. His wife stood by his side, unmistakable in her beauty, her face the inspiration for bard's tales for leagues. Someday, Afric could have a woman like that—bought and paid for with his father's gold.

Piers de Montgomery stared at him too long and Afric realized he was waiting for him to speak. "Indeed," he said, and raised another toast. "To you and yours, good sir."

Lyon Montgomery smiled. So did Afric as he took a heaping swig of *uisge*—the only good thing to come out of these Highlands as far as he was concerned. But he must be careful not to overindulge, or he'd end up once again in a pile of limbs. Moving slowly away from Montgomerie, he watched Page and waited for the opportunity to strike...

MALCOM SCOWLED, WATCHING THE REVERIE WITH indignation. Amid laughter and drink, his warnings were already forgotten, but he wasn't so much angry as he was frustrated. Perhaps his Da had reason to question his intuition, but Malcom had very good reason not to give his trust so freely.

At the tender age of six, he had very nearly become a prisoner of the English crown, abducted by his own uncle from his bed, then bartered to the English. That he was a free man was in no small part due to the piggishness of Page's mean-old father, who'd valued his king over the love he'd born his daughter. And yet, not once had Page ever spoken a cross word about him, despite that Malcom had spent enough time at Aldergh to know how little he'd valued her—which was to say, not at all. The oaf had ignored Page, leaving her to sup at the lower tables in his hall. In fact, he'd sooner given Malcom a seat at the high table—the son of his enemy—whilst his daughter scraped her morsels from the bottom of the pot.

All in all, Hugh FitzSimon had treated his daughter more like the daughter of a servant. Malcom felt sorry for the girl she had been, but fortunately for her, she was beloved by all and Malcom had no cause to worry about Page at all.

Peering over his shoulder, he watched as his father took her by the hand, luring her away from the celebration, and a tentative smile returned to his lips, pleased to see them so happy, even after all these years.

But more importantly, with his father's attention now on his cherished wife, Malcom was free to follow his gut... he didn't need any of his father's men. He could search the woodlands alone.

Perhaps the fire had been an accident. Perhaps it might have been rotten luck, but something about the entire situation raised Malcom's hackles.

Coincidentally—or perhaps not so coincidentally—the flames had remained clear of the MacLean woodlands. It left them untouched, despite being so close, and how fortuitous, he thought—particularly since it left a perfect hiding place in full view of their village.

No matter what his Da believed, his sense of foreboding had little to do with the company they were keeping— strangers though many might be.

Something truly was amiss.

And now, with or without his father's blessings, he intended to discover what it was. At twilight, when the darkening sky descended into the treetops and the fire's glow swallowed the light of the sun, he slipped into the woods, none the wiser, leaving the sound of music and laughter in his wake. As Glenna had said he must do, he let intuition be his guide...

CHAPTER 5

S tocked to the rafters, with supplies covering the light from the windows, the barn was utterly dark. It was little wonder Constance and Kellen had found their way here. With so much work to be done, this was perhaps the last place they should be, but it had been a good long week or more since Iain had availed himself of the treasure his wife was hoarding. Abstinence was driving him mad.

"Iain, *mo dhuine...*"

My man.

His Scot's tongue flowed easily from her tongue, sweet as syrup, but he knew she was about to protest, and he pressed a finger to her lips. "Shhhh, my love. Say no more."

At thirty-one, Page was little older than he had been on the day he'd met her, but unlike his own hair, her beautiful tresses had yet to show a trace of gray. The only lines she wore on her face were laugh lines about her lips—sweet, sweet, bonny lips that pleasured him so well throughout the years. He was more in love with her now than ever.

"Iain," she protested as he drew her further into the stable, setting her against a wall. "We have guests."

Murmuring his appreciation for all she did, he slid a hand down her waist, skirting her warm, soft thigh and his lips curved mischievously as he put a hand to her rear.

"Whatever has come over you?" she asked. "I thought you said you had something to show me?"

"I do have something to show you," Iain said hungrily. "I truly do." And he did mean to show her the bounty of gifts they'd been given, but at the moment he was obsessed with a kiss. He pressed his lips against her mouth, telling her, "I've a terrible craving for plums."

She sounded perplexed. "Plums?"

"Aye," he said. "Plums."

"*Céadsearc*," she said. *My first love.* And her softly spoken endearment put a yearning betwixt his legs. "You'll find no plums beneath my skirt," she said huskily.

Inhaling the sweet scent of his wife, ignoring the predominant scents of their barn, Iain pulled Page close, his cock hardening beneath his plaid. "I disagree," he said. "That's where I should find the most delicious plum of all. I *know* that plum... I've dreamt of that plum... I long to sink my teeth into its tender flesh, lift my tongue along the cleft..."

In answer, Page shivered in his arms, and Iain knew instinctively by the way she melted against him that his fingers would find her wet and ready. He was utterly intoxicated by the scent of her, and the feel her...

He was no longer a boy, she no longer a girl, but she was as beautiful today as she was on the day he'd met her, dressed in so little, with her hair sopping wet.

Page—his heart, his love—had given him so many years of loyalty and love.

"No one will miss us," he coaxed. "On the other hand... you have *my* undivided attention." And he pressed himself against her, so as to make his point.

Her eyes widened, so, too, did his grin.

. . .

"You are Incorrigible!" Page complained, and yet, even despite the complaint, she lifted herself onto her tiptoes to kiss her husband's beautiful mouth. She slid her arms about his waist, capitulating even as she protested.

"*Cèol mo Chridhe, Keh-ole moe chreeyeh*," he said. *You are the music of my heart.*

Reason returned slowly, but it did return.

Her husband was a master puppeteer, knowing her only too well. But they had a houseful of guests, a wedding to see to, and that was only if you somehow managed to forget that they had a village to rebuild. With so much work to be done, this was *not* where she should be right now. She put a hand to Ian's chest, firmly, but gently pushing him away.

"Alas, my love, there are too many people," she said, giving him a chastening glance.

Resigned, he pouted like a child, then sank his teeth into the hollow of her neck and Page shrieked, then laughed. And all the while, he ravaged her neck, sending gooseflesh across her body, she wanted to drag him down to the ground. Because, in truth, she cared not one whit that the earth might be cold, or that the smell of pigs and horseflesh surrounded them. At times like this, she was again that young lass who'd loved her champion so fiercely...

As he nibbled her collar bone, alternately nipping and kissing, Page reveled in the familiar scent of the man wrapped in her arms. It was so easy to see how young folks could get carried away... but then... she detected other scents... scents that were not suited to a stable. Cinnamon. Ginger. Lavender. Cloves. Page froze.

"Iain?"

Her husband stopped kissing her all at once, responding to the tone of her voice.

"Did you order supplies to be stored in the stables instead of the storehouse?"

"What?"

"It's dark," she said. "Light a lamp."

" Now?"

"Yes, now." She had a very sudden sense of peril. But before either of them could regain their senses, she heard the crack of metal against bone and felt Iain stumble against her.

CHAPTER 6

Any sense of chagrin Page might have suffered over having been caught in the midst of kissing her husband fled at the sight of Iain sprawled in the dirt.

The stranger had emerged from the shadows, hitting him hard enough to leave him for dead, then dragged Page out of the stable, screaming in protest.

No one heard her.

Unlike the night before, all work had ceased. In honor of Kellen and Constance, her husband had declared this a day of celebration, so everyone was now at the bonfire, half a league away—purposely constructed as far from surviving structures as possible.

"We can't leave him!"

The man—dressed in MacLean red—jerked Page's arm so hard that it made her squeal.

"He'll be fine," the stranger declared, "I merely smacked him on the head, but if ye make me go back, I'll make sure he won't rise again."

Page's relief was palpable. "You have no inkling what you have done. My husband will search for me and he *will* find you," she warned, and then she wished she hadn't made such a boast. The last thing she wanted was for him to go back and make sure Iain was dead.

The man chuckled darkly, and his accent was strange. "He won't find you 'til 'tis too late."

Page had a sinking feeling in her gut. "Too late?" She struggled against his hold on her. "Too late for what?"

She couldn't place his accent—not precisely—but it was vaguely familiar. But he wasn't Scots.

"Because your father is going to kill you," he explained, sounding entirely too pleased by the notion.

Page was genuinely confused. Her father had had nothing to do with her for ten years and more. "Hugh is here?"

"Aye."

"With you?"

"Not precisely."

"Why has he come to kill me?"

"Does it matter?"

Page bristled at the question. "Of course it matters!" Once again, to no avail, she struggled against his hold on her.

What child ever wished to believe her father could do her harm? Hugh FitzSimon had never loved her overmuch, but she couldn't imagine him coming to murder her in cold blood. And still ... he'd been quite willing to discard her. It made her heart wrench that he might actually want her dead. But why? What could he hope to gain?

Page was no son, and therefore she would never inherit her father's demesne. In terms of politiks, it was far more reasonable to assume he'd pass his legacy to a bastard son. Had not King Henry's illegitimate son, Robert of Gloucester benefited this way?

"Who are you?" Page demanded to know.

"Someone with a vested interest in Aldergh."

Aldergh?

Suddenly, she remembered a kitchen maid with the same accent, and she remembered her father smacking that woman on the arse. Who was this man?

Now that they were far enough away, and Iain wasn't in immediate danger, she planted her heels, refusing to budge.

The stranger dragged her across the field, against her will. The light of the bonfire and ringing of voices diminished as he pulled her in the direction of the woods.

A sliver of a moon lit the twilight sky, but it lay half hidden behind a bank of puffy white clouds, giving the landscape a grey, otherworldly light.

With every step she took, Page expected to hear her husband calling for her, but the sound of Iain's voice never emerged from the stable, and the merriment fell further and further behind...

'Who are you?" She demanded again.

The man jerked her forward when she tried to sit. "Who I am is not important."

"Someone *will* notice I am gone," she warned him, remembering another time she'd made such vain threats. And yet, this time, Page knew beyond a shadow of doubt that her husband and clan valued her. This time, someone *would* come once they realized she was gone. These were her people, and they would never sit idly by, allowing this miscreant to take her life. "They'll come after you, they *will* find you and they will kill you."

"Nay," the man said confidently, once again jerking Page by the arm. There was glee in his voice. "They will find your father's camp and then they'll blame Hugh. And when they find him and kill him, I'll be gone."

A tiny spark of hope flared—not because this man meant to harm her, but because clearly her father must not be the one behind this atrocity. Still, she wanted to know, "Why is my father here?"

"Because that bag of wind believes he can buy his way to heaven by rebuilding a few hovels."

Page's heart thumped against her ribs.

Her father was the one who'd rebuilt their huts?

Her brow furrowed, catching a whiff of the man's horrid scent, and then suddenly she remembered those odors in the stable... scents from her past—lavender, cinnamon and cloves. The cloves she still smelled on the man dragging her away—a tincture precisely like the one that kitchen maid had used to mask her body's scent.

She'd had a son, and Page had wondered if his father was a fish because his mother smelled so horrible. The woman claimed her son had a noble sire, and then one day he vanished... and suddenly she knew. She knew who he was, and she guessed why he was here.

Page swallowed, hard. "I *know* who you are."

The man jerked her arm again and said, "Shut up."

Peering over her shoulder, Page searched for help, but there was no one. And judging by the growing silence, her husband had never emerged from the stables. Her heart squeezed with fear. No one seemed to realize what was happening, and her father—wherever he might be—was in danger as well.

If Iain should happen to find Hugh first, and Page didn't have the chance to explain—or if Malcom or Cameron discovered him before Iain did, they would kill him on sight.

"What makes you think you'll get away with this?" Page asked furiously.

"Shut up," the man said again, and Page grit her teeth.

"I don't want Aldergh," she said. "What makes you think it could ever be mine?"

"If Matilda should happen to seize her father's throne, she could easily rule in your favor, because she's a bitch."

Page screwed her face. "Matilda?"

"Henry's Empress daughter."

"I know who she is! What has she to do with anything? Henry is the one who will decide!"

The man laughed hideously. "Stupid little bitch. Henry is dead."

Stunned, Page nearly tripped as they slipped into the woods. *Henry was dead?* She would be too if she didn't extricate her from this mess—and her father as well!

Peering over her shoulder one last time to gauge the bonfire's distance, she decided she had more to lose by keeping silent. She whipped about and screamed her father's name at the top of her lungs.

CHAPTER 7

Hugh was quite pleased with himself.

Half his men were gone. The other half were still at camp, busy packing the last of their gear while Hugh took a piss.

The ride south would be far less cumbersome without the wagons, but at least the weather was still warm.

Somewhere out there, his daughter was eating, drinking and dancing, and wouldn't he love to stay to see it, but alas, there was no use lingering where they might be found. His men had warned him there was talk about interlopers amidst the clansmen, and that young Malcom was out snooping about. If the boy should happen to venture into these woods, he'd most certainly discover Hugh's camp, and he didn't relish a repeat of past circumstances.

Of course, he wasn't *that* man anymore, and he felt badly about wringing that poor dog's neck—and about embroiling Cameron MacKinnon into his machinations. But done was done, and he couldn't change the past. He could only affect the future, and to that end, he sighed contentedly, because, at long last, his work here was done.

Eleanore, his sweet Eleanore, had given him a vision of what his legacy would be and then could be. She'd shown him the fate of his life and death, and the bonfire now lit was the flame she had spoken of—the flame that should not die before his work was done.

Last night, after stashing the last of their offerings into the MacKinnon's stable, they'd stolen MacLean cloaks and snuck in to finish rebuilding what homes they could. Now it was past time to go—before the celebration ended and the drunkards went stumbling home.

Hugh remembered only too well how stout their *uisge* could be, and yet, it wasn't stout enough to keep those Scots bastards from drawing their swords.

Hopefully his daughter would discover his gifts and someday realize what he had done. Until then, it was enough to know that Eleanore knew he'd made amends. Now, he could rest at ease that his legacy might continue after he was dead.

Suddenly, he dropped his tunic.

"Hugh!" shouted a woman. "Hugh FitzSimon!"

Could it be Eleanore? But nay... she had not reappeared to him since that evening at Aldergh.

He yanked up his trews.

The forest was getting dark now, with no sign of that strange blue aura he'd spied the night at Aldergh. So it wasn't Eleanore. Instinctively, although he knew not how or why, he sensed it must be Page, and as though to prove his point, she called him again, very nearby.

"Papa!" she screamed, and the sound of that single word twisted Hugh's heart.

For an instant, he felt a rush of excitement. Could it be that she'd already discovered his gifts and she'd come to beg him not to go—*an old man could wish, could he not?*

Dashing through the woods, toward the sound of his

daughter's voice, he realized as he went that it wasn't a happy shout.

Something was wrong.

Snatching his bow from the sling on his back, he plucked out an arrow from his quiver, then skidded to a halt, his bow and arrow poised in his hands. "Afric," he said, with no small amount of surprise.

"Hello father."

MALCOM HADN'T GONE FAR INTO THE WOODS WHEN HE HEARD the scream.

"Hugh!" shouted a woman. "Hugh FitzSimon!"

Instinctively, he withdrew his sword from his scabbard, the sound a hiss in the night. Without hesitating, his feet began to move, running toward the sound. And then, he stopped abruptly as he spied the outline of a man standing in the shadows, bow in hand. Malcom slid behind a pine tree for cover, realizing the man was so preoccupied he hadn't heard him. The stranger was wearing mail—English, he surmised—holding a bow with a nocked shaft, taking aim, drawing back...

His eyes followed the path of his arrow and located the man's target, and it took him a full moment to realize precisely what was happening. He'd known something was amiss, and here was proof... Hugh FitzSimon held an arrow aimed at his daughter, rearing back, ready to let it fly.

The fact that she was struggling against another man didn't immediately strike Malcom as it should have.

There wasn't time to consider. All Malcom knew was that the woman who had raised him was in her father's sights, and if he didn't intervene, right now, Hugh FitzSimon would finally kill her after all these long years.

Malcom was close. All he had to do was rush the man. He had a sword in his fist and the fire of vengeance burning in his heart.

Completely without fear, he lunged after FitzSimon, his sword finding purchase in his back, straight through his heart. But FitzSimon had already loosed his arrow. It happened too swiftly. Page screamed again. Malcom saw only in that instant that the arrow must not have been intended for her. It went straight through her captor's head, felling the man at her feet. Page gave a sob, and ran straight into her father's arms as he crumpled to the bracken.

Confused, Malcom stood, watching the scene unfold with disbelieving eyes.

"PAPA," SHE SOBBED.

Hugh was more than aware that his blood was spilling into the cold, wet earth, but he rested easily, knowing his arrow had found its mark. That was one thing the years could never wrest from him: Even as his legs had failed him, and his belly fattened, he could still wield a bow.

"Papa," she cried, her lips quivering with emotion.

Hugh had always loved that about her—the fact that she loved so freely, even when it wasn't returned. Eleanore had been that way as well as well—even until the end.

His sight dimming, Hugh squinted up at his only daughter—the beautiful woman she had become—confused by the turn of events. Afric was dead. Hugh was dying. It wasn't supposed to happen this way. He'd only meant to help. He furrowed his brow... hadn't Eleanore said he would have another chance?

In that instant, the forest light took on a strange blue hue and suddenly everything seemed so clear.

The second chance wasn't for him. It was for his heirs. As

for Hugh, this would be his end. But strangely, he wasn't afraid. He was only cold, intensely cold...

Another pair of wide-blue eyes peered down at him, this pair over his daughter's shoulder. "Malcom?" he said, recognizing the handsome, young face no matter how old the boy had grown. "Ye're a fine, fine lad," he said. "Any man would be fortunate to have you as a son."

And these were his last words.

"Hang on, papa. Hurry, Mal! Go get your father," Page commanded. "You'll find him in the stables. Hurry, please go!"

Hugh's breath came more labored. The sound of his own breathing came amplified to his ears while Page's voice drifted away. She was sobbing—poor, poor girl.

The sound of her grief hurt his heart, which seemed to be beating all the more slowly now. He heard crispy leaves rustle as Malcom dashed away, thinking that he would love to have a boy like that as his heir.

Realizing he was nearly out of time, Hugh struggled to remove the ring from his swollen finger. This was all he could give Page now, his legacy. She was Aldergh's rightful heir.

He managed to remove the sigil ring, pushing it wordlessly into her hand and tried to speak, but tinny blood gushed up through his parched lips.

"No, no, no, no...." Page shook her head. "Papa," she pleaded so brokenly. "Oh, papa... I love you, Papa." He heard her say, over and over, like a litany in his head. "I love you, Papa," she said, and he recognized the truth in her eyes—she loved him still—even after all these years—even after all he had done. Words refused to form on his lips and still, he opened his mouth in an attempt to speak.

I love you, he longed to say, and closed his eyes, recalling Eleanore's words: *You will know love when 'tis returned.*

With his dying breath, his heart burst with joy.

And then he saw her—his wife—seated beside the hearth fire, dressed resplendently in red, and wearing his cloak. The room was brightly lit, and Hugh was no longer cold. He stepped tentatively into the solar.

Eleanore smiled at him, a radiant smile that put to shame the fire raging in the hearth. There was nothing frightening about her now. She was beautiful and welcoming.

"You did not die alone," she said, her voice like music to Hugh's ears.

"I did everything you said," he told her, still confused.

Eleanore rose from the chair and came to take him by the hand, her gaze full of love as she enveloped him in her arms. Warmth and forgiveness filled him, from his head to the very tips of his toes.

"My dearest love," she said, "I never promised you longer life. I but gave you the gift of knowing and a chance to make amends and perhaps change the hand of fate."

"What happens now?"

Somewhere, in the place Hugh had left, his daughter wept for him still. The sound lingered faintly at the back of his head, like a distant memory. He peered back at the doorway from whence it seemed he must have come. Out, beyond the solar where he now stood, in what should have been the hall, remained a forest that was growing darker by the second.

Eleanore turned her hand, begging him once more to take it. "I hear tell Henry has arrived. Shall we go?"

Henry? The old bugger!

But all trace of jealousy had fled, no longer doubting Eleanore's love. In another life, he might have moved his mouth to ask where they would go, but he had no need of voice here. He already knew. He took Eleanore by the hand, and together they flew...

EPILOGUE

Aldergh Castle, Northern England 1137

Page reined in her mount, sidling up to her laird husband, and sat for a moment, taking in the sight of her father's legacy—hers now to bestow.

What irony there was in that?

Her father was dead now, but with his dying breath, Hugh FitzSimon had given her everything she'd ever longed for. Three small words, and a sigil ring she intended to give to Malcom. She longed to ease the tensions between the men in her life, but if Malcom didn't accept her behest, these lands would be forfeit, returned to the English crown, and there was no one else to hold them in her father's stead.

Twelve years had gone by since she'd left, wherein she'd vowed never to return... but here she was now, and Aldergh Castle appeared much the same as it had the day she left, save for a small footbridge her father must have installed after widening his moat.

Page had every faith that once Malcom wrested control of the castle, Stephen would cede him the baronetcy, if for no other reason to lessen the number of barons prepared to do battle against him. Later, if Matilda managed to take her rightful place, Page would intervene again, petitioning on her son's behalf.

The cavalcade had settled well outside of missile range, still close enough to make out banners. Flying against a vivid sea of red, her father's two-headed falcon whipped with the breeze. Malcom seized the flag from his banner-man, and held it aloft. News would have preceded them by now, but until they faced those men who held this garrison, they could not anticipate how this might go.

The countries were at odds now. Henry of England was two-years dead and Stephen of Blois had seized Henry's throne. Matilda had challenged him. They'd only waited so long to see who might prevail, but they could delay no longer, or Aldergh would be forfeit to the crown.

A single horn blast trumpeted across the landscape and from this distance they could see men rushing over the ramparts, tiny black forms scurrying between machicolations.

Page laid a hand atop her belly, only slightly bumped, and smiled a secret smile. As yet, not even Iain realized, and she hadn't told him yet because she knew he would never have allowed her to come—not when they were facing the possibility of a siege. Unfortunately, she realized her presence was crucial, and there was a part of her that desperately longed to ride again through those castle gates.

The last time she'd set eyes upon her childhood home, she'd been naught more than a girl, far too willful to remain locked behind those walls—much to her good fortune. The stars must have aligned for her that day, for that was how she'd met her husband—after sneaking out to take an evening swim. If she but closed her eyes, she could see him now standing before her as he had that day, the silver at his temples, rivaling the glint of a setting sun.

"Catching glowworms perchance?" she'd asked, because he'd stared too long, mouth agape. She'd been captured in her chemise, wet and looking like a stray.

"Bones o' the saints," he'd said. *"'Tis no wonder your da lets you run aboot in the middle o' the night. He's like to be hopin' ye'll lose your way in the dark."*

There had been such truth to his words, and his barb had wounded her. No one ever cared so much where she went, or what she did, until the day she left this place.

Would they care now that she had returned?

Her son trotted up beside her, ready to do battle.

Acutely aware of her husband's disapproval, she nevertheless proceeded to tug her father's ring off her finger, relinquishing the heirloom, offering it up for Malcom in her palm. He seemed to hesitate, and Page could only guess at his thoughts.

That day in the woods, after he took her father's life, all trace of his youth fled from those stark green eyes. Pensive, and full of purpose, there was naught left of the boy in him now. He was far more brooding than his father had ever been and if he didn't leave their fold, he would wither and die beneath the fury of his ire. "You have the writ from King Stephen and my father's ring," she reassured. "It will be enough."

Nodding, Malcom took the ring from her palm, and Page gave him a warm, reassuring smile, hoping it would make up for her husband's disappointment. "Put it on your small finger, Malcom. And remember... what happens from the moment you ride through those gates determines how they will receive you. You are Aldergh's new lord now."

Up on the ramparts she could see the watch signaling for the portcullis to be raised.

Malcom peered at her with a question in his eyes. "Art certain, mother?" he asked.

"You *are* my son," she told him.

Even as young as he was, Page had every faith he was ready to embrace this destiny. God willing, her husband would have many years remaining. In the meantime, Malcom was no longer fated to build his legacy in his father's shadow. Page studied him, seated atop his horse—his dark golden hair ruffling in the morning breeze.

"Let us be done," his father said gruffly.

Malcom straightened his spine, raising his banner high. "Aye," he said. "Let us be done." And then, without a word, he spurred his mount forward—a boy become a man.

Page and Iain shared a glance, and then fell into place behind him, moving swiftly toward the opening gates.

Dressed in her father's cloak, and wearing his sigil, Malcom *Ceann Ràs—hot head*—as they'd begun to hail him, rode in before them. Cantering along behind him, Page rode across the moat and into the familiar bailey.

"Welcome home, Lady Aldergh," someone shouted up at her, lifting her heart.

And then another, "Welcome home!"

One after another, her father's kinsmen hailed her as she passed them, familiar faces welcoming her.

Page sat straighter in the saddle. No more was she that nameless child, for whom nobody had cared. And, in truth, she didn't need her father's legacy to feel esteemed, and nevertheless, one by one, they gave her obeisance, falling to their knees. Tears swam in her eyes.

Welcome home.

She heard the last greeting whispered at her ear as the wind blew the curls of her hair. Her father's voice. She felt him in her heart. *Welcome home,* he said.

Welcome home. Welcome home.

A NOTE FROM TANYA...

Dearest Reader,

Through the years, I've gotten countless emails from readers lamenting the lack of an epilogue for The MacKinnon's Bride. Many reviews also shared that sentiment. But at the time I wrote The MacKinnon's Bride an epilogue simply didn't fit the story. So why an epilogue now, after all these years?

In part, I wrote it for you. In part, for me—I wanted to revisit these characters and see them living happily. But if you're also following along in the Guardians series, you know these books are connected and take place about the same time. The new epilogue serves as a bridge to an upcoming story in a brand new series... maybe you'll guess who it's about?

One thing I will tell you: If you follow medieval history, you know the proverbial brown stuff is about to hit the fan. King Henry of England dies on December 1, 1135, plunging England into civil war. Stephen of Blois is crowned on December 22, on the eve of the Winter Solstice, and he will spend the next nineteen years until his death defending his throne against Henry's daughter Matilda. My next historical series, Daughter of Avalon, will take place during this tumultuous era.

Turn the page to read a preview of the upcoming The

King's Favorite. It's a bit of a departure for me, but one that won't be much of a surprise now that you've read this slightly magical epilogue. Please note: It is not necessary to read either The MacKinnon's Bride or MacKinnons' Hope to enjoy The King's Favorite, but why not since both are FREE for a limited time—my gift to you. Happy reading!

Tanya Anne Crosby

ABOUT THE AUTHOR

Tanya Anne Crosby is the New York Times and USA Today bestselling author of thirty novels. She has been featured in magazines, such as People, Romantic Times and Publisher's Weekly, and her books have been translated into eight languages. Her first novel was published in 1992 by Avon Books, where Tanya was hailed as "one of Avon's fastest rising stars." Her fourth book was chosen to launch the company's Avon Romantic Treasure imprint.

Known for stories charged with emotion and humor and filled with flawed characters Tanya is an award-winning author, journalist, and editor, and her novels have garnered reader praise and glowing critical reviews. She and her writer husband split their time between Charleston, SC, where she was raised, and northern Michigan, where the couple make their home.

For more information
Website
Email

Newsletter

Made in the USA
Monee, IL
30 January 2023

26694092R00059